Dear Parents,

Welcome to the Scholastic Reader series. We have taken over 80 years of experience with teachers, parents, and children and put it into a program that is designed to match your child's interests and skills.

Level 1—Short sentences and stories made up of words kids can sound out using their phonics skills and words that are important to remember.

Level 2—Longer sentences and stories with words kids need to know and new "big" words that they will want to know.

Level 3—From sentences to paragraphs to longer stories, these books have large "chunks" of texts and are made up of a rich vocabulary.

Level 4—First chapter books with more words and fewer pictures.

It is important that children learn to read well enough to succeed in school and beyond. Here are ideas for reading this book with your child:

- Look at the book together. Encourage your child to read the title and make a prediction about the story.
- Read the book together. Encourage your child to sound out words when appropriate. When your child struggles, you can help by providing the word.
- Encourage your child to retell the story. This is a great way to check for comprehension.
- Have your child take the fluency test on the last page to check progress.

Scholastic Readers are designed to support your child's efforts to learn how to read at every age and every stage. Enjoy helping your child learn to read and love to read.

　　　—Francie Alexander
　　　　Chief Education Officer
　　　　Scholastic Education

Copyright © 2003 by DC Comics.
Batman and all related characters and elements
are trademarks of and © DC Comics.
All rights reserved. Published by Scholastic Inc.
SCHOLASTIC, CARTWHEEL BOOKS, and associated logos are
trademarks and/or registered trademarks of Scholastic Inc.

Library of Congress Cataloging-in-Publication Data

Grayson, Devin K.
    Batman: the copycat crime / by Devin Grayson; illustrated by
John Byrne.
        p.   cm. — (Scholastic readers. Level 3)
    "Cartwheel Books"
    Summary: When the Riddler kidnaps the son of a police detective,
Batman comes to the rescue.
    ISBN 0-439-47097-8 (pbk.)
    [1. Kidnapping — Fiction. 2. Heroes — Fiction. 3. Police — Fiction]
    I. Title: Copycat crime. II. Byrne, John, 1950–   ill. III. Title IV. Series
    PZ7.G79915Bar 2003
[E] — dc21   2003004929

10 9   06   07

Printed in the U.S.A. 23 • First printing, September 2003

BATMAN
THE COPYCAT CRIME

Written by **Devin Grayson**

Illustrated by **John Byrne**

Batman created by Bob Kane

Scholastic Reader — Level 3

Cartwheel
·B·O·O·K·S·®

SCHOLASTIC INC.

New York   Toronto   London   Auckland   Sydney
Mexico City   New Delhi   Hong Kong   Buenos Aires

CHAPTER ONE

MISSING PERSON

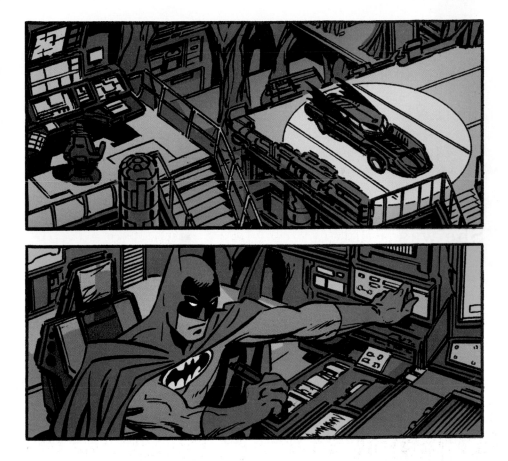

Bruce Wayne was one of the richest men in Gotham City. He lived in Wayne Manor, above a secret cave — the Batcave!

That's because Bruce was also Batman!

Every evening Batman carefully checked his crime-fighting tools and equipment. Tonight he was almost ready to go out on patrol.

Meanwhile, young Brian Fletcher was checking his math homework. Brian lived on the other side of Gotham City.

He looked at his watch. It was dinnertime. But Brian's mother wasn't home yet. She was a detective. Many nights she came home late.

Brian went to the refrigerator. He took out the peanut butter, the jelly, and the bread. He made two sandwiches. Brian poured himself a glass of milk. Then he sat down to dinner alone.

Two hours later, Detective Fletcher walked into her house.

"Brian!" she called.

But Brian didn't answer.

Detective Fletcher went into the kitchen. She saw a plate with crumbs and an empty

glass of milk from Brian's dinner.

"Brian!" she called again.

Still, no answer. Detective Fletcher ran into

Brian's room. On his bed, she found a note. It read:

What is the tallest building in Gotham City?

"A ransom note in the form of a riddle!" cried Detective Fletcher. "That could only mean...the Riddler!"

Detective Fletcher called her captain. "The Riddler has kidnapped Brian!" she cried. "I found a riddle on Brian's bed. It said: What is the tallest building in Gotham City?"

"The tallest building in Gotham City is the Wayne Enterprises building," said the captain. "I'll get some squad cars over there right away. Meet me there!"

CHAPTER TWO

RIDDLE ME THIS

BRIAN WAS *NOWHERE* TO BE FOUND.

Six squad cars surrounded the Wayne Enterprises building. All night long, the police officers searched the building. But Brian was nowhere to be found.

After twenty-two hours, Brian was still missing. Detective Fletcher met with Commissioner Gordon.

"Please find my boy," she begged.

"We're doing everything we can," said the commissioner.

A third voice added, "And we'll do more." Detective Fletcher jumped at the sound. She thought that she and the commissioner were alone.

Then someone stepped out from the shadows of the alley. It was crime fighter Batman.

"We need your help, Batman," said Detective Fletcher. "I found this note on my son's bed. We've searched every inch of the Wayne Enterprises building, but we haven't found him."

Batman looked at the note. "This looks like the work of the Riddler."

"That's what we thought," said the

commissioner. "But the Riddler was in jail when it happened."

CHAPTER THREE

A DOUBTFUL DUO

"We've asked the Riddler to help us find Brian," the commissioner said to Batman.

The commissioner led Batman and Detective Fletcher to a police car. The sly Riddler was inside. "Hello, Batman," the villain grinned. "Why is seeing you today like taking a vacation?"

"I don't know," said Batman. "But what do you know about Brian Fletcher?" He held up the riddle about the tallest building.

The Riddler laughed. "Is that the riddle you need me to help you solve?" he asked.

"It's the only clue we have," said the commissioner. "The answer is the Wayne Enterprises building. But we didn't find the boy there."

"You won't solve this if you think like a grown-up," said the Riddler.

"What do you mean?" Batman asked.

"The kid wasn't kidnapped," said the Riddler. "I bet he ran away from home. He's the one who wrote that riddle."

"Do you know where we can find him?" asked Detective Fletcher.

"No," said the Riddler. "But I'd be happy to look!"

He kicked out the screen between the front and backseats. The screen hit the driver in the head. The driver slumped over.

Batman tried to stop the Riddler.
But the Riddler was too fast. He climbed
into the driver's seat. Then he sped off,
shouting, "Why is seeing you today like
going on vacation? Because it means I can
get away!"

CHAPTER FOUR

GUESS WHO?

MEANWHILE AT THE LIBRARY...

Brian was bored. He was sitting in the large reading room of the Gotham City Public Library. He counted the lights on the ceiling. He counted them again. He looked at a stain on the wall. He pretended it was a dragon. Then he pretended it was a dinosaur.

Brian was feeling lonely. And he was feeling scared. Suddenly he heard a crash.

He jumped to his feet. Maybe his mother had figured out his riddle and come to get him.

"Mom!" he called out. He rushed to the door. Then he stopped.

Instead of his mother, he saw a man. The man wore a mask and a green suit. The suit was covered in question marks.

"What's the tallest building in Gotham City?" asked the Riddler. "The library is the tallest building because it has so many stories!"

Brian stepped back. "Are you the Riddler?"

The Riddler grabbed Brian's arm. "Yes, I am," he said. "And now that I'm here, you're really being kidnapped."

Brian tried to pull away. But the Riddler held on tightly.

BRIAN **STEPPED BACK**.

"They let me out of jail to help find you," the Riddler said. "But they'll want to put me back. You're going to help me stay out of jail!"

"Please," said Brian. "I want to go home!"

"You should have thought about that before you ran away," said the Riddler. "Why did you do it?"

"My mom says it's her job to follow clues and catch bad guys," said Brian. "She spends more time with them than she does with me. I wanted Mom to look for me instead of other people."

Still holding on to Brian, the Riddler wrote two notes. He put one on a reading table. He placed the other in a big book.

"Batman will catch you," Brian told the villain. "He's probably figuring out my riddle right now. He'll be here soon."

"I'm sure he will," said the Riddler. "That's why we have to hurry up — and leave!"

CHAPTER FIVE

FRIDAY BEFORE THURSDAY

Batman had indeed figured out Brian's riddle. He rushed to the library with Detective Fletcher and the commissioner. There Batman quickly found and read the Riddler's two notes.

"Meet me at the Gotham City Stadium," he told the detective and commissioner.

And then he was gone. How did he know Brian and the Riddler would be at the ballpark? Detective Fletcher read the first note. "Where does Friday come before Thursday?"

She spotted a dictionary on the table. Batman had left it there. Then she knew the answer to the riddle.

"Friday comes before Thursday in the dictionary!" she said.

Batman had left the dictionary open. A second note was taped under the word "Friday." The commissioner picked it up.

He read the note out loud. "Riddle me this. Your boy is worth more than gems to you. But is he worth more than the biggest diamond in Gotham City?"

"The biggest diamond in Gotham City,"

said Detective Fletcher. "Batman thinks
he means the baseball diamond at the
stadium!"

"Let's go!" said the commissioner.

CHAPTER SIX

FULL COUNT

The ballpark was mostly dark. But lights shone on home plate. Brian was standing on the base.

Batman walked toward Brian.

"Stop!" Brian shouted. "The Riddler said something bad will happen if I step off the base."

Batman stopped.

"The Riddler also told me to tell you a riddle," Brian said. "Does it take longer to run from first base to second base or from second base to third base?"

Batman carefully walked toward

second base. He looked at the ground. "It takes longer from second to third base," he said, "because there's a 'shortstop' in the middle."

Batman walked between second and third base. He bent down and dug up the

dirt. He saw a red wire. Batman took a clipper from his utility belt and cut the wire. "Whatever booby trap the Riddler set won't work now!"

Just then, Detective Fletcher ran onto the field.

"Brian!" she cried.

Brian called back. "Mom!"

Batman nodded to Brian that it was now safe for him to leave the base. And Brian ran to his mother.

Commissioner Gordon joined them. "I guess we lost the Riddler," he said.

"He's at the lighthouse," Brian said.

"Did he tell you where he was going?" his mother asked.

"No," answered Brian. "But while he set the trap, he made me a bet. He bet that I couldn't guess which building in Gotham City weighed the least."

"Good work, Brian," said the commissioner.

"I'm on my way to the lighthouse," said Batman. "The Riddler will be back in jail by morning."

Before he left the stadium, Batman asked a riddle. "When things go wrong, what can you always count on?"

"Your family?" said Detective Fletcher.

"Batman?" said Brian Fletcher.

"Your fingers!" said Batman. Then off he went.

BATMAN *RACED OFF TO* THE LIGHTHOUSE.

And the next day, as Batman promised, the Riddler was back in jail—but for how long?

THE RIDDLER WAS BACK IN JAIL...

...BUT FOR HOW LONG?

Fluency Fun

The words in each list below end in the same sounds.
Read the words in a list.
Read them again.
Read them faster.
Try to read all 15 words in one minute.

clipper	checked	building
commissioner	kidnapped	ceiling
driver	searched	everything
fighter	slumped	morning
officer	walked	something

Look for these words in the story.

refrigerator	detective	library
villain	dictionary	

Note to Parents:

According to *A Dictionary of Reading and Related Terms*, fluency is "the ability to read smoothly, easily, and readily with freedom from word-recognition problems." Fluency is necessary for good comprehension and enjoyable reading. The activities on this page include a speed drill and a sight-recognition drill. Speed drills build fluency because they help students rapidly recognize common syllables and spelling patterns in words, and they're fun! Sight-recognition drills help students smoothly and accurately recognize words. Practice these activities with your child to help him or her become a fluent reader.

—**Wiley Blevins**,
Reading Specialist